Hi. My name is Katie.

This is my Mommy, my Daddy,
my little sister Molly, and my baby brother John.

This is Meme. Meme is my Daddy's mother and she has Alzheimer's disease. That means that her brain doesn't work as well as it used to.
You can't catch it like a cold, and you can't see anything like when someone has chicken pox.
Only older people can get Alzheimer's but not all do, and some people get it worse than others.

When Meme first got Alzheimer's I couldn't really
tell anything was wrong. Sometimes when she would come
to visit she'd call me Molly or forget what she was
talking about -- but sometimes even Mommy does that.

One day Meme was at our house and she tried
to help Mommy by washing the dishes. When she
was done they were still dirty, but Mommy didn't
want to hurt Meme's feelings so Mommy waited for
Meme to leave and then she rewashed everything.

Another time Meme went to the store and got very lost. She was really scared and didn't go out by herself much after that. Mommy and Daddy would help Meme food shop and take her places she needed to go, but there were too many things Meme still needed help with.

After a while, Mommy and Daddy decided it would be
better if Meme came to live at our house. I thought
this was a great idea. At first we had lots of fun.
Meme would play with John and Molly and me.
We would watch TV together and color.

Every night before bed Meme would read us a story
and give us each one of her special hugs.

One night while reading us our favorite story,
Meme seemed to have trouble reading some of the words.
She said she probably just needed new glasses.
This was okay with me because I got to
help Meme with some of the words.

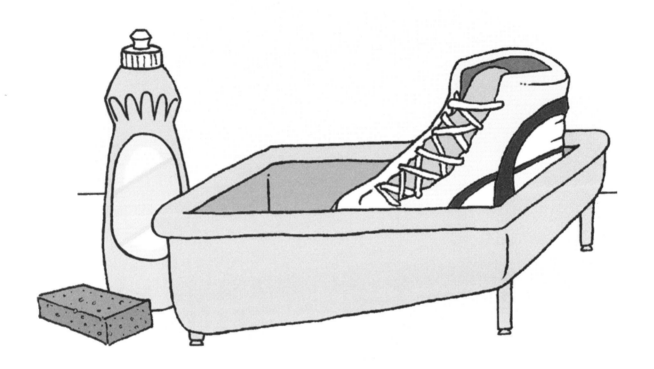

Meme started doing a lot of funny things,
but I never laughed because I knew she wasn't trying
to be funny. One time she washed one of Daddy's
sneakers in the kitchen sink. She used dish detergent
and a sponge and left it in the dish drainer to dry.

Another time she put John's diaper on backwards,
but she was only trying to help and it was
still fun having her with us.

I remember when Meme started saying she was ready
to go home. I tried to tell her that she was home and I even
took her to her room and showed her some of her things.
She didn't understand me and just looked sad.

I went and told Daddy what had happened and he explained
to me that each day Meme's brain was slowly stopping.
He quickly put one of Molly's puzzles together and showed
me how as time goes by Meme would keep losing pieces
of the puzzle. The pieces don't come back or heal like
when I skinned my knee and once these parts of
Meme's brain stop working she wouldn't be able
to think as well as she had before.

Meme started to want to go home so much that she would
pack her suitcase and leave. Sometimes she'd walk really
far and Mommy would have to go look for her in our car.
It's not that Meme didn't love us, she just wanted to
go home -- only she didn't know where home was.

Then there were days when Meme didn't know who we were.
I remember one time she asked, "Who is the mother of these
children and how can she leave them alone like this?!"
Mommy didn't want to confuse Meme or upset her
so she said, "She'll be back soon."

Meme started being angry a lot. She never used to get mad but now she seemed mad all the time. This hurt my feelings. Mommy explained that I didn't do anything wrong. Meme was just having a bad day. She still loved me but some days she was really confused and it made her angry and scared.

I know I get angry when I get confused,
like when I'm trying to a read a new book…
But Mommy or Daddy always help me figure out
the new words, and I always feel better.

Sometimes I was able to help Meme remember things, and when I couldn't I would think of something else to talk about. I had to be as patient with Meme as I had to be with Molly and John. Just telling Meme I loved her always made her feel better, and it always got me a big hug. Sometimes a hug was easier than words.

We put special locks on all the doors to keep Meme safe and we bought her a special bracelet with her name and our address on it in case she got lost.

Meme started having a lot of bad days and we learned that if
she was busy she'd be happy. Sometimes Mommy would
bring Meme stacks of clean towels to fold and Meme would
fold them over and over and over again. Daddy would bring
Meme lots of change to sort for him. Once Molly pulled all
of the tissues out of the box and Meme refolded everyone
of them. Mommy had a box full of buttons and I liked
to sit and help Meme separate them by color or by size.
It made Meme happy to feel like she was helping us.

Meme liked to sit and look at her old picture books and sometimes she'd listen to her music tapes. She wasn't angry when she was busy and I was so glad to be with her.

One day Meme got out and she took John with her.
She said she was taking her baby home.
It took a while but Daddy brought them back inside.
Mommy was really upset.

Daddy decided it was time to put Meme into a Nursing Home. This was a special place where all the other people were like Meme. The special nurses there would know lots of ways to keep Meme happy and we could visit her anytime. I was sad when it was time for Meme to go but she just couldn't live at our house anymore.

Sometimes when I visit Meme she knows me
right away and some days it takes a few minutes for her to
remember me. Other days I'm not sure if she remembers
me at all. I hope she does. I always bring her a special
present that I make for her myself. When it is time to leave
I give her a great big hug. When I'm hugging Meme
all that matters is how much I love her.

BENJIE

ON HIS OWN

JOAN M. LEXAU

BENJIE
ON HIS OWN

Illustrated by DON BOLOGNESE

THE DIAL PRESS NEW YORK

To Benjamin of course from Aunt Joan

Benjie waited and waited.

"That Granny," he said. "Why don't she come?"

School had started a week ago. Granny was there every day when school was out. But not today.

He didn't want Granny coming for him in the first place. "I'm too big for that," he had told her. "I can go to school and back by myself. And I can play outside without you always watching."

"Not on these streets, child," Granny had said. "It isn't safe for you to be on your own yet. Lots of folks go for their children after school."

That was so and Granny had made her mind up for sure. Benjie put up with it.

Now he said, "I don't think Granny's coming. Well, I'll show her I can go home by myself."

He walked to the corner and looked around. Granny had always been with him so he never had to think about which way before. There were a lot of corners to turn, he knew that. But not which way to go!

And why wasn't Granny here? Benjie started to worry. Granny would have come if she could.

Some big boys were playing ball in the school playground. One of them was a boy from Benjie's street.

"Hey, Ray!" Benjie yelled.

Ray came over. "What you want?"

Benjie knew his face was red. This was a hard thing to say. "I don't know the way home," he said. "Granny didn't come. Can you take me home?"

"What a baby!" Ray said. "O.K., you wait, kid. Soon as the game is over, I'll take you." He walked away.

"Hey—" said Benjie. He had to go home now to see if Granny was all right. But Ray was running after the ball.

Benjie felt like crying. Only he wasn't going to let Ray see him cry.

He turned around, looking this way and that. Down one street was a candy store. That was where Granny got him his crayons for school. It was on the way home. Benjie went that way. When he came to the corner, he looked all around. Ahead of him was the hot dog wagon. He went by it every day after school.

He walked faster and faster.

Benjie was scared he wouldn't find the way home. He was even more scared about Granny. "There must be some big trouble or she would have come," he said to himself.

He started to run.

There was a sound behind him. He looked back. A great big dog was coming after him. "Oh, no!" he said. He ran faster. "Go on home!" he yelled at the dog.

The dog ran faster.

A little girl yelled, "Junior. Junior! You come back here." The dog turned and went back to the girl.

At every corner Benjie looked all around for things he had seen before. From one corner he saw a big church. At the next corner it was a purple bike chained to a tree.

A few big boys were down the street. They looked at him in a way he didn't like. He started to cross the street. But he didn't have a chance. The boys were all around him. "Going to the store for your mother, boy?" a tall boy in dark glasses asked.

He wanted to say, "What's it to you?" Or, "You let me be." Or, "Don't call me boy like that."

There were a lot of sayings in his mind, but he didn't let them out. The thing he cared most about was getting home fast to see how Granny was.

Benjie looked down at his feet and shook his head. "I'm going home from school," he said.

A boy with striped pants said, "He hasn't got any money."

"Make him turn his pockets out," the tall boy said.

Benjie turned his pockets inside out. They could see he didn't have any money. They looked at his arm to see if he had a watch.

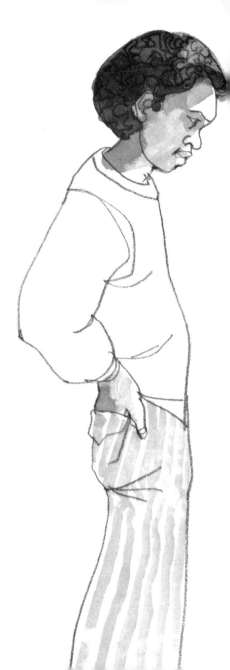

Benjie tried not to think how scared he was so he wouldn't cry or try to run. He knew he couldn't run as fast as these big boys.

"What shall we do with him?" a fat boy asked.

Benjie looked at him. "Let me go home, please," he said. "I think my grandmother is sick."

"Baby wants his grandmother," the tall boy said.

"Oh, shut up!" said the boy with the striped pants. "Maybe his grandmother is sick. Go on home, kid."

"Next time you come around here, have some money with you," the fat boy said.

Benjie ran. At the corner he turned and looked back. They weren't coming after him. He was safe.

He started to cry now, but he made himself stop. He didn't have time
for that. He saw he was near home. He knew the way from here.

At the next corner he looked up. There was the lady in the window on
the second floor. She was at her window every time Benjie went by. She
looked down at him as she always did. But she didn't smile. She never
smiled at him. Sometimes Benjie smiled at her but not today.

He turned the corner and ran by the fish store.
And there was his building. He ran up all the stairs.
On the fifth floor was the room where he and Granny
lived. The door was locked and Granny had the key.

"Granny!" he yelled. He was crying a little now. "Granny, you home? You all right?" He pounded on the door.

Granny opened the door. She was holding on to a chair to stand up. Her face didn't look right.

"I'm awful sick, Benjie," she said. "I couldn't go down all those stairs. I been sitting in this chair by the door, praying you'd get home all right."

"What you want me to do, Granny?" Benjie asked.

"The Atkins aren't home," she said. "I yelled at their window. See if you can get somebody to phone for an ambulance."

"I will, Granny," Benjie said. He helped her over to her bed. She held on to him on one side and the chair on the other.

Benjie went out and pounded on doors. Maybe somebody in the building had a phone. But nobody was home. Or they were scared to come to the door. Granny never went to the door if she didn't know who it would be.

He ran outside.

There was a phone on the corner. But he didn't have a dime. No use asking Granny for one. They had potatoes for supper last night, so he knew Granny was out of money again.

Anyway he didn't know how to work that phone. And Granny had tried to call on it a few times and it was never working.

"Hey. I could use that other phone. The police phone," he told himself. Granny had said it was for people to use when they were in trouble. Granny was sure in trouble now.

Benjie ran to the phone. But he couldn't reach it. He began to climb. At first he fell down a few times. But then he was just about up to the phone. He put his hand out to open the box.

Somebody pulled him down and yelled, "What are you up to, dummy? And why did you tell me you didn't know the way home from school when you did? I been looking all over for you, you crazy kid."

It was Ray.

Benjie said, "I didn't know the way home. And let me be, dummy. I got to call for an ambulance. My grandmother is sick."

"Why didn't you say so?" Ray said. "Here, I'll help you up."

Benjie picked up the phone and said into it, "Hello? Can you send an ambulance?"

"What's the trouble, son?" a policeman asked. "And where do you want the ambulance to go?"

Benjie told him where. "I don't know what Granny's sick from but she's awful sick," he told the policeman.

The policeman said, "All right, son. You have somebody wait by the door of your building to show the ambulance men the way. They'll get there as soon as they can. O.K.?"

"O.K.," Benjie said. He ran back to his building and stood by the door for a little while. "I can't stay down here," he said. He had to go up to Granny. She was so sick and all alone.

The ambulance might take a long time. He remembered when Ray's brother had been hit by a car. It took an hour for the ambulance to come. The ambulance men had said they were busy. There were too few ambulances in that part of the city, they said.

Maybe Ray would wait for the ambulance so he could go up to Granny. But Ray was gone. There was no one he could ask to do it.

Yes, there was. "I'll ask that lady who always sits by her window," he said out loud.

He ran around the corner. If the ambulance came now, he could hear the siren and run back in time.

Good. She was still there.

"My grandmother is sick. Could you wait by my building for the ambulance—" he began.

But she shook her head. "I can't walk," she said. "I can't go out. I'm sorry."

"Oh," Benjie said. "Sorry." He ran back to his building.

He had to go see how Granny was. Maybe she was sicker. "I'll run upstairs and come right down," he said. "No, the ambulance might come just then and go away."

He didn't know who else to ask. He knew the faces of some of the people on his street but not many names. He didn't even know the names of most of the people in his building. Granny said hundreds of people lived on each block. It was too many people to get to know.

"If I could just get somebody to wait for the ambulance here," he said. But how? What would Granny do? Granny sometimes said, "When you can't think what to do next, pray. And then think harder."

So Benjie prayed. First he looked all around. God was all over, Granny had said, so he could look any which way when he prayed. But Benjie didn't feel right looking just one way when God was every place.

"God, I need help. Granny is so sick but I have to stay here," he prayed. "And I don't know how long that ambulance will take."

Now it was time to think harder.

And then it came to him. There was one thing he could do. He didn't want to do it. But what else could he do?

He opened his mouth and yelled as loud as he could, "HELP! Please somebody HELP!"

He yelled and yelled. After a long time people looked out their windows. "What is it? What's the trouble?" a woman yelled.

"My grandmother is sick—" he began.

All the heads went away. They didn't care. They just didn't care that Granny was sick! What could he do now?

"God, I still need help," he said, and at last he really cried, harder and harder. He had done all he could.

But then he could hear the man at the fish store yell, "Hurry, Mrs., never mind with the apron. The little boy's grandmother is sick."

Mrs. from the fish store came running. Her apron was half on and half off. "Where is the grandmother?" she said.

"Fifth floor," he said. "It's 5D. But I—"

She was on her way up the stairs. Well, maybe she would know how to help Granny. He didn't. So he'd stay down here.

Then he saw that people were coming out of buildings all along the street. Even his building. From down the block, he saw Ray coming with a woman. They all came over to him.

"I went home to get my mother to help," Ray said.

Some people came from around the corner. "Where is the boy with the sick grandmother?" a man asked. "A woman around the corner yelled at us from her window. Said a boy here had a sick grandmother and needed help."

Ray and some men stayed down to wait for the ambulance. Benjie told them how to get to his room. A lot of women went upstairs with Benjie.

He saw that Mrs. from the fish store was packing things in a shopping bag for Granny to take to the hospital. He helped her find some of the things. With all the women wanting to help Granny, Benjie had a hard time getting near her.

Then he didn't know what to say. She had her eyes shut and he just looked at her. He wasn't with her long before the ambulance men came.

He stood back so he wouldn't be in their way.

But before they took Granny away, she asked for him. All the people pushed each other back to make way for him.

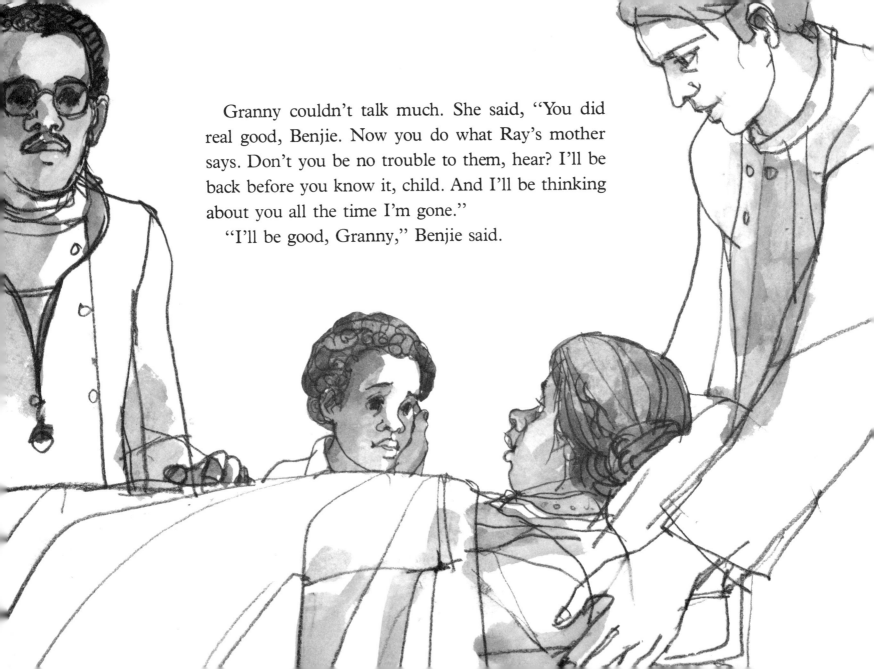

Granny couldn't talk much. She said, "You did real good, Benjie. Now you do what Ray's mother says. Don't you be no trouble to them, hear? I'll be back before you know it, child. And I'll be thinking about you all the time I'm gone."

"I'll be good, Granny," Benjie said.

Benjie watched as they took Granny away. She was looking at him with worry in her eyes.

"Granny!" he yelled. He wanted to say, "Wait for me." But he stopped just in time. He knew he couldn't go to the hospital with Granny. Saying he wanted to would just be more trouble for her.

So he yelled, "Don't you worry about me, Granny. We both be all right, you hear?"

One of the ambulance men turned and said, "That's right, son. Don't you worry about this old lady. We'll take good care of her."

Benjie knew what Granny was going to say.

"Who you calling an old lady?" she said crossly to the ambulance man. Granny was trying to cheer him up. Benjie laughed loud so she could hear.

The ambulance went away.

"That siren sure makes a sad sound," Benjie said.

Ray's mother said, "Come on home with us now, Benjie. Later I'll call up and find out how your Granny is."

So Benjie went home with them. When Ray's mother called the hospital, they told her Granny would be in the hospital a few weeks. She would have to take it easy for a while after that.

"But she'll be all right. That's the big thing," Ray's mother said.

The next morning at breakfast Benjie did some thinking. What was going to happen after school? Would Ray's mother take him? Or Ray? But Ray went with friends as old as he was. They wouldn't want Benjie along.

"I can get to school by myself. The same way I got home yesterday," he told himself. "I don't need anybody to take me."

But he kept thinking about those big boys on that one street. And that great big dog. He didn't want to go near them alone again.

Maybe he could find another way to walk to school.

"Hey, Benjie, that was funny when all those women were yelling about you," Ray said.

"When?" Benjie asked.

"Over at your place," Ray said. "When the ambulance came. All those women yelling they'd take care of you. They were getting mad at each other. Didn't you hear?"

Benjie shook his head. He had been busy trying to get out of the way of the ambulance men then.

"Well, Momma won when she said I'd walk to school and home with you," Ray told him. " 'Like a big brother,' she said. Your granny said you'd like that. She said, 'He's getting to be a big boy. But I worry about him so.' " Ray smiled. "My momma was just like that when I was littler."

Benjie grinned.

"Oh, well," he said, "when Granny gets home I guess I'll let her take me to school again. That should make her feel better."

Ray laughed. "And you too I bet. Come on, you crazy kid, we'll be late for school."